Raves for the "Foreigner" series:

"Cherryh's gift for conjuring believable alien cultures is in full force here, and her characters ... are brought to life with a sure and convincing hand."
— *Publishers Weekly*

"A seriously probing, thoughtful, intelligent piece of work, with more insight in half a dozen pages than most authors manage in half a hundred." — *Kirkus*

"Close-grained and carefully constructed ... a book that will stick in the mind for a lot longer than the usual adventure romp." — *Locus*

"A large new Cherryh novel is always welcome ... a return to the anthropological science fiction in which she has made such a name is a double pleasure ... superlatively drawn aliens and characterization."
— *Chicago Sun-Times*

"As always, Cherryh alternates complex political maneuvering with pell-mell action sequences in an intensely character-driven SF novel sure to appeal to the many fans of this series." — *Publishers Weekly*

"Her lucid storytelling conveys enough backstory to guide newcomers without boring longtime series followers. The characters are well drawn, and Cherryh's depiction of both human and alien cultures is riveting."
— *Library Journal*

"... transforms the book int
of anthropological SF and '
Faithful Foreigner saga follo
a ball."

C. J. CHERRYH
INTRUDER

DAW BOOKS, INC.

DONALD A. WOLLHEIM, FOUNDER

375 Hudson Street, New York, NY 10014

ELIZABETH R. WOLLHEIM
SHEILA E. GILBERT
PUBLISHERS

http://www.dawbooks.com

First Printing, March 2013
1 2 3 4 5 6 7 8 9

DAW TRADEMARK REGISTERED
U.S. PAT. AND TM. OFF. AND FOREIGN COUNTRIES
—MARCA REGISTRADA
HECHO EN U.S.A.

PRINTED IN TIIE U.S.A.

To Jane, for always being there
and always coming through.

1

Spring in the southwest, and the heavens had opened—not the gentle rains of the summer, but a sheeting deluge that warped the spring landscape beyond the tinted windows of the bus.

Inside, warm and dry, working on a tray table almost sufficient for his paper notes, Bren Cameron enjoyed a sip of tea from a scandalous plastic cup. He had the four-seat executive arrangement to himself at the moment, and his briefcase lay open on the adjacent seat. His four-person bodyguard had all gone to the rear of the bus to converse with the young contingent of Guildsmen they'd been handed for protection, and that left him room to work.

Lightning flashed just uphill from the bus. Thunder cracked—worrisome for electronics, but he wasn't working on his computer this trip. That machine had far, far too much in its storage to be bringing it into Taisigi territory, and he'd sent it on to the capital with his valets and significant items of furniture, the computer itself to be hand carried and guarded every step of the way. The spiral-bound notebook was enough for him, along with a stack of loose-leaf work and printouts and, within the briefcase, a folder of very official papers, vellum with red and black wax seals and carefully preserved ribbons.

A dark presence moved down the aisle, loomed over him and switched out the vacuum-thermos teapot on his little work surface. Jago was not a servant—the sidearm attested to that. So did the black leather of the Assassins' Guild. She stood a head taller than any tall human, black-skinned, golden-eyed—atevi, in short, native to the world, as humans were not. She was half of the senior pair of his atevi bodyguard—a bodyguard, and his lover, moderately discreetly, of some years now.

He was the sole human on the bus, a single individual of fair hair and pale skin and pale civilian dress in a company of black-uniformed atevi. He was the sole human on the mainland, by now, and his personal world had gotten back to the atevi norm, where he looked up at everyone he talked to and struggled with steps and furniture. He was not a small man—as humans went. But here, even a small teacup meant a generous pouring, and the seat he occupied, scaled for atevi, accommodated human stature with a footrest.

It was his bus. And it had such amenities. He was dressed for court, lace at the cuffs and collar, a pale blue vest. His coat, beige brocade, hung behind the driver. He had his fair hair braided, and the ribbon that tied that braid was white, the badge of the paidhi-aiji—translator for the aiji, the ruler of the aishidi'tat, the Western Association. The white ribbon meant peace and nonviolence, the paidhi's job being that of an intercessor in the affairs of lords.

The white ribbon was supposed to mean peace and nonviolence, at least, and the gun he usually carried in his pocket was in the luggage this trip. The bulletproof vest was only a precaution.

Jago made a second trip forward to advise him, leaning on the seat back across the aisle. "We have just crossed the border, Bren-ji."

The border out of Sarini Province, that was.

So they were now in Taisigi district, in what had been hostile territory for centuries—a place he never would have contemplated entering. Not on his life.

But he'd already been there. He'd negotiated with the lord of the Taisigi. He'd gotten out in fairly good shape, despite the efforts of some.

And he was coming back, to finish what he'd started,

now that the Assassins' Guild had taken "supportive control" of Tanaja, the capital of Taisigi clan.

"Will you want lunch, Bren-ji?" Jago asked him. The galley on their well-appointed bus was in operation. A pleasant aroma had informed him of that some while ago.

"A light one, Jago-ji, half a sandwich, perhaps." There was no knowing whether they were going to attend a formal dinner tonight—or a firefight. Although the odds were considerably against the latter, one still never quite bet on anything, not where it regarded the lord of the Taisigi . . . who had just a little reason to be upset about recent events. "Have we made contact yet?"

"With the Guild, yes," Jago said. "Not yet with Lord Machigi's staff."

"Let me know when you have, Jago-ji."

"Yes," she said, and went back down the aisle.

He poured another small dose of tea, sipped it, reflexively saved his papers from a spill as the bus hit a hole, and took a fleeting note: *Road improvement, Targai-Najida to border*—for a time when relations might be easier. They were still on the Sarini plateau, but the road—which on the atevi mainland meant a strip of mud, gravel, or mowed grass leading somewhere the railways didn't go—would start descending hereafter, headed for the heart of the Marid, an arm of the wider sea that was its own small world.

The Taisigi whose lord he proposed to visit were one of the five clans of the Marid.

Lord Machigi of the Taisigin Marid had become the last man standing of the three most powerful Marid lords. The three lords had plotted, each in his own way, to take over the west coast of the aishidi'tat; unfortunately, one Bren Cameron, whose country estate lay on the West Coast, on Najida Peninsula, had decided to take a vacation right in the middle of the territory in question.

The Marid, immediately seeing something ominous in his presence, had attempted to assassinate him and his young guest, Cajeiri—who happened to be the eight-year-old son of Tabini-aiji, the ruler of the aishidi'tat.

That had brought in the lad's great-grandmother, not the quiet sort of great-grandmother, but the lord of the East and *not* the power to cross if one wanted a long life.

Hence the paidhi's current trip to Tanaja, in a shiny red and black bus, with his own bodyguard and ten junior Guildsmen. His bodyguard hadn't been sure the juniors were an asset—more apt to need protection than to provide it, in Jago's words; but they were the guard the Guild had come up with on short notice, the Guild having deployed almost all its senior assets in the recent Marid action, and when all was said, ten additional Guildsmen with equipment certainly looked formidable.

So the younger contingent came along—in case absolutely everything he'd worked out with the young lord of the Taisigi had gone to blazes overnight. Which, in the volatile politics of the aishidi'tat, was not impossible.

Go talk to Machigi, the aiji-dowager had said—Ilisidi, the aiji's grandmother and young Cajeiri's great-grandmother. Get Machigi to give up his claim on the West Coast and ally with us. In turn, we shall stop the Guild from assassinating him. That was the order that had sent him to Tanaja the first time.

So ... in the upshot of it all, two Marid lords who hadn't won Ilisidi's favorable attention were now dead, their houses occupied by the Assassins' Guild, who were busy going through their records and finding out a host of things the deceased lords would not have wanted published to the world ... or to their own clans.

And here he was back in Lord Machigi's territory for the second time in two weeks. Machigi's premises were also being occupied by Guild forces, but in a theoretically benevolent way.

Tabini-aiji, back in the capital of the aishidi'tat, in Shejidan, was still watching the operation in some curiosity—rather in the manner of one watching two trains run at one another, as Bren saw it. Tabini could have vetoed the notion. He hadn't. He'd let his grandmother run the operation, backing her up as needed ... and possibly intending to let any adverse events bounce back on Ilisidi, not on him.

But Ilisidi's plan was apparently still going smoothly.

The potential in the situation had been damned scary for about three very unsettled days, in which the Assassins' Guild in the capital had met to consider a massive operation against a sizable portion of its own membership—a faction of the Assassins' Guild which, three years ago, had overthrown Tabini's rule for two significant years and then fled the capital when Tabini had come back on a wave of popular support. The Assassins that had supported the usurper, Murini, had run south ... and reorganized.

Worse, Guild internal secrecy had covered the problem. It had covered it so damned well that not even Tabini-aiji had known—because Tabini, who had replaced his Guild-approved bodyguard with men of his own clan, who were not high up enough in the Guild to suit the Guild leadership ... had somehow fallen off the list of persons to be informed of certain maneuvers.

Politics, politics, politics. The Guild had started running its own operation, trying to mop up their recent split, not advising Tabini of everything it knew—

Like the fact that the splinter group had moved beyond organizing in the Marid—that they had turned the two northernmost lords of the Marid into puppet lords, putting the two clans at *their* direction.

Tabini still hadn't been told, because his bodyguard, who should have informed him, had ties and relatives not approved by the Guild leadership.

The aiji-dowager's bodyguard hadn't been told, either—first because she was in close company with the aiji, and second because she had been a guest of a lord with notoriously lax security, who might innocently have blown the Guild operation.

So secret were the inner workings of the Guild that the paidhi's high-ranking bodyguard hadn't been told, either, and *his* bodyguard contained at least one person who was tapped into the Guild at highest levels. Algini, partnered with Tano, had reasonably expected information he hadn't received.

Why not? Because *his* lord, the paidhi-aiji, was working closely with Tabini and the aiji-dowager, and somebody high up in the Guild was in the final stages of planning a strike against the renegades in the south and was absolutely not confiding in the messy households of people who actually lived lives outside the rules of the Guild, and who were running around near the sphere of action at the time.

And what then happened?

The Guild's enemies tried to assassinate the paidhi-aiji, because he'd walked into *their* operations, unadvised.

Then they'd gone on attacking, because the aiji-dowager and Tabini's young son had added themselves to the target zone.

Just run over to Tanaja and get Machigi to join us . . . that had been Ilisidi's approach to the situation that had landed on them at Najida.

And that had tripped up the Guild's maneuvering for good and all, since Machigi had been the first target the Guild had been putting the pressure on.

An ignorant intervention?

One didn't quite think so. The *hell* Ilisidi's bodyguard hadn't started to get information that the Guild hadn't been willing to give to Tabini, once bullets had started flying, and the *hell* the aiji-dowager hadn't made threats and promises to get it out of them—the aiji-dowager's chief bodyguard, Cenedi, probably allying with Algini to get accesses. The paidhi-aiji knew the smell of politics when it wafted past him. Cenedi had started finding things out, and then *Algini* had started finding things out, as the machinery started to move.

Now the Guild in Shejidan had the shadow-Guild on the run. The average citizen in the northern Marid might know that his own lord had died, yes. That they were also missing a minister or two might take longer to notice. The sudden appearance of uniformed Guild in the halls of government would be the only sign—and that would get to the flower market and the fishmonger by the city rumor mill . . . that and certain government offices opening under the direction of lower-level officials, senior officials having had the sense to resign and go tend their personal business . . .

That was the pattern in Senji clan territory, north of here, the other side of the Maschi district. It was the same across the Marid Sea, in Dojisigi clan, where most of the shadow-Guild had clustered—and where some of the nastiest fighting had gone on.

The Guild had told Tabini, finally; the Guild had been in communication with Ilisidi, and right now the paidhi's bodyguard was in radio contact with the Guild authority, and everybody was talking to everybody else.

Going into Taisigi territory was still a scary proposition. But it certainly beat the last trip. He had packed hiking boots this trip. He'd sworn to himself he would never go anywhere again without hiking boots.

And—theoretically—this time the Guild would courteously warn them if they were heading into a trap.

He had his lunch while lightning broke around them, while from time to time the windshield went awash with water. It was a typical spring front, coming in off the straits. But with luck, the worst of the weather would blow past them and be off across the Marid Sea by the time they got to Tanaja, on the coast.

Meet with Machigi and then call and arrange a secure flight from the airport over in Sarini Province, a bus ride back to the airport, and on to Shejidan. For business. A lot of business.

His guests had all departed from Najida. Young Cajeiri had flown back to Shejidan yesterday—Tabini-aiji had insisted on a plane flight, no more train rides. Young Dur had flown his own plane home yesterday, too, ahead of the storm. Dur's father, going home by sea as of two days ago, would have had a rougher trip, at least at the outset.

Ilisidi and her security team would have taken off hours ago, just ahead of the incoming front, the last of his guests to leave. She would change planes at Shejidan, not delaying for pleasantries, and continue on to her own estate, Malguri, across the continental divide. She was taking Lord Geigi's traitorous nephew Baiji with her—under close guard. Baiji was a fool, but he had his uses—primarily in begetting an heir.

Lord Geigi himself was still over at Kajiminda, the estate neighboring Najida, lingering to straighten up some last-moment business there, before catching the next shuttle back to the space station and getting back his real job.

So the construction crew would be moving in tomorrow to repair Najida's main hallway and the roof with more than the patches that currently kept the rain out. And to do some major renovation while they were at it.

He loved that little estate. He wanted to stay and supervise the construction and be consulted for small decisions.

But he had a promise to keep. And a duty to perform.

And if he succeeded, the world would change.

2

It was going to be goodbye for good to the little bedroom in Great-grandmother's apartment, and Cajeiri was not happy. It had been home ever since they had gotten back from space, but where they were going next was their real home ... which they had not been able to go back to until now.

It was repaired, since the coup. The bullet holes were patched. It was repainted.

But in Cajeiri's view, his room there was going to be only one more room in the Bujavid.

Where Cajeiri had rather not be in the first place.

He had only been infelicitous six when he had last seen his parents' real apartment in the Bujavid.

Oh, it was a fine place, the Bujavid. His father had his offices and his audience hall here. Here the legislature sat, and here was the national library. Here almost all the most important lords lived when they were in town, and the halls were full of important and historic things, and all that.

But his father's newly painted apartment was so—clean. So white. So—modern. He had had a look through the doors yesterday, only that. And it was just—white. Which was actually the way he remembered it, from long, long ago.

He had only really lived in that apartment when he was a baby. He had, since then, lived in Great-uncle Tatiseigi's house; and then he had gone up in the shuttle and lived on the starship, and he had flown on the starship farther than anybody on earth could imagine; and he had traveled back to the space station—which he had had to leave in a hurry, leaving all the people he had met in space.

And then he had flown back down to the world with nand' Bren and Great-grandmother, because his father had been overthrown and enemies were in control of the capital, and they—he and Great-grandmother and Father and nand' Bren—had had to fight their way from Uncle Tatiseigi's house back to the Bujavid again and set his father back in power.

So he had come to live in this room, in Great-grandmother's apartment, which had stayed safe during the Troubles. His father and his mother had lived here, too. And he had been almost a whole year living in this warm little bedroom. And taking lessons from his incredibly boring tutors—well, except for one small incident. Or two.

His father had of course become aiji again, so his father was obliged to live in the Bujavid and, as soon as he could, to have his own apartment back. They were cramped, living with Great-grandmother.

But *he* had rather live with Great-grandmother or with nand' Bren, which was where he had just been—at Najida—even if he had only gotten to go out in a boat once.

Well, twice, if one counted the accident. But that had not exactly been a proper boat.

And everything was better at Najida now, and just when there was a real chance nand' Bren could have taken him out every day on his boat, or nand' Toby could have—his parents wanted him back in Shejidan, and told him he had to fly home.

Great-grandmother had gotten to stay in Najida. And now she was coming back, but she was not even going to come in from the airport. She was taking that fool Baiji to meet the girl he was going to have to marry.

So he did not even get to see her.

And now everybody was running around in excitement because they were moving back to their own apartment, as if that was good news.

They were moving there tomorrow.

And that was where he would have to live.

Forever.

With a boring tutor giving him boring lessons.

He had ever so much rather have his lessons from Great-grandmother, even if she did thwack his ear for mistakes.

Or from nand' Bren, who had taught him all sorts of things.

Or from Banichi, who was Guild, and incredibly scary and very kind and understanding. Those were his best teachers. Ever.

When they had been on the starship, nand' Bren had given him vids from the human archive, about dinosaurs and musketeers and horses. He never got those any more. He scarcely ever got to spend time with nand' Bren and Banichi.

And worst of all, Great-uncle Tatiseigi was back in residence in the Bujavid, now, and they would probably have to have dinner with him once a week once they had a dining room.

Then his mother's Ajuri clan relatives were coming in, because the legislature was about to meet, and they would take *any* excuse to come visit. The aunts were not so bad. But Grandfather was appalling.

Mother was about to have a baby, that was the problem. That was a lot of the problems. The Ajuri were all excited about it, as if his mother did not already have *him*. They were probably saying that *this* baby would never be exposed to nand' Bren, and they would far rather a baby that *they* could rule—

They would certainly rather have somebody *they* could influence. He had had far too much to do with Great-grandmother and with humans. That was what they thought. He was sure of it.

Great-grandmother would come back when she had gotten Baiji married off.

But by then he would have moved out of this apartment, with his parents, with all sorts of rules.

In *their* apartment, he would have a whole lot of *their* staff watching him. A lot of his parents' staff who had not been killed in the coup had been off on paid leave since his father had come back to power because there was just no room for them in Great-grandmother's apartment.

But his father's staff would be all over the new apartment, and he would not be able to make a move without somebody reporting it to his father or his mother.

It was just dismal.

Pack, they had told him. Or would you rather the servants did it?

He most certainly did not want the servants going through his things. They would hardly know what was important. The things they could handle were in the closet—which was a lot of clothes—and what was not clothes was in the boxes on the floor, which were his drawings and his notes.

And then there were the important things in his pocket, where he kept his slingshota, along with three fat perfect rocks from Najida's little garden, which he never ever meant to shoot where he could lose them. They were more precious to him than anything but the slingshota itself.

It was not very much to own for somebody who was the heir of all the aishidi'tat. But it was all he really cared about keeping. Not counting the clothes. Which he personally did not count. The servants could move those.

He was just short of his felicitous ninth year, and in one more day he was going to be miserable for the rest of his life.

He had his own bodyguard now, at least: Antaro and Jegari, who were not Guild yet, just apprentices. They were sibs, from Taiben, and they were almost grown, but they understood him better than anybody in the Bujavid.

And now there were Lucasi and Veijico, another

brother and sister team, who were real Guild and carried weapons and wore the black uniforms and everything. His father had assigned them to him. His father was not thoroughly pleased with them ever since Najida. But they had learned a lot, and improved. So they were his, and he would not let them go.

His parents had promised him his bodyguard would have rooms of their own in the new apartment. And he would have a little suite. Which was good. He had not even been interested in looking at it when he had had a chance to look in on the apartment.

They had told him no, there would be no windows where they were going, not in his suite; he had not been surprised, but he was not happy about it, either. Ever since coming back to the Bujavid, he had felt closed in. Mani's apartment had not just a window, but a whole balcony you could sit on. But his father's bodyguard would not let him go out there.

So for the rest of his life, he would just have to sit in his windowless little suite and do homework and ask the servants to do anything that was remotely interesting. He had wanted this morning to go to the library and look up things about the Marid, because he had gotten interested in it, but his father's bodyguard would not let him out of the apartment.

That was a forecast, was it not? It was just what things would be.

He was bored and angry, and went disconsolately from one thing to another. He tried to read the book nand' Bren had lent him and wished he still had the vids from the ship that he had grown up with.

He wished even more that he had his companions from the ship, humans his age. He really wished there were someone, anyone, his age that he could talk to. But he was the aiji's son, and who got to be associated with him at all was a political question, and important, and so far there was no boy his age in the whole world that his father approved of.

And if ever his father approved, he still had to get his

mother to approve, and Great-grandmother, and Uncle Tatiseigi, and his Ajuri grandfather.

It was just grim here.

And it was going to be grim. Forever. His mother and his father and his grandfather and Uncle Tatiseigi had his whole life planned.

He sat down at his little desk, took a pad of paper and a pen, which had come with the desk, and, still furious, drew Najida estate the way he remembered it. He put in the rocks at the turn of the walk that led down the hill to the harbor. He put in nand' Bren's boat, and nand' Toby's. He ran out of paper for the little rowboat he had borrowed.

He ruined that, and drew it again on another sheet of paper. He constantly tried to draw things, to remember them when he had to move again. And he kept his drawings secret, among his Important Things, in that box on the floor.

Then it occurred to him he should draw this room, because once he had moved out, there was never any guarantee he would be back, or that the room would stay the way it was, once he had no say in the matter. So he drew it next, the tassels on the bedcover, the desk he was using, the hangings on the wall, the tapestry with the picture of a boat, and, most important, his big map of the whole of the aishidi'tat.

Veijico knocked and came in. "Nandi. A message from your mother. She wants you."

Damn, he thought. And thought it twice. And again. He was not supposed to say that word out loud even if it was ship-speak and nobody had any idea it was swearing. Damn. Damn. *Damn.*

Maybe it was a security lecture coming. His father had already had the security lecture with him. The legislature was going into session and there were controversial bills going to be on the floor, which brought out crazy people, who had any citizen's right to be on the bottom, public floor of the Bujavid, so he must remember that.

And there could be people who were much more

dangerous than simply crazy. There could be elements of the renegade Guild that they had not caught yet. The shadow-Guild, nand' Bren called it. And *they* were scary.

So he was supposed to stay in the apartment.

He knew about defense. He had been with mani and Cenedi and nand' Bren and Banichi over at Najida, in all the shooting. He had defended the house, had he not? He had defended mani.

And those people had been armed and bent on killing everybody.

He had killed somebody—more than one somebody in the course of things, though it upset him to think about it, and he sometimes dreamed about it; he did not want to say that to his bodyguard, whose job was to save him from situations like that. He had things he remembered and kept all to himself. Grown-up things.

But his parents never gave him credit for knowing anything at all.

He had no choice about going to his mother, now, however. He got up and put on his coat, with Veijico's help, and when he went out the door of his room, the rest of his aishid was waiting for him. They were probably curious, being as bored and shut-in as he was, and with the same things ahead of them. So they were going to go with him and watch him get in trouble. He hardly blamed them. But:

"You can all stay outside," he said, annoyed with it all. "One expects a security lecture. And you know all of that."

"Yes," Antaro said, speaking for the aishid; so they would stand outside the door, waiting for details.

His mother, three doors down the hall, didn't have any of her bodyguard on duty ... what with her guard, and his father's, and his, the bodyguards all bumped into one another in the halls, and his young aishid had their own hard time, dealing with senior Guild, whose business was always more important and who always got the right of way.

He reached his mother's door, and Antaro knocked, once.

His mother's major d', Lady Adsi, opened for him and let him into his mother's borrowed little sitting room.

"Your mother is expecting you, young gentleman," Lady Adsi said, and left him to stand there facing nothing in particular while she disappeared through the inner door of his parents' suite.

In a moment more his mother came through that door. She was very pregnant, but she was always beautiful. Today she had on a blue drapey coat and a lot of blue and white lace, and she smiled at him. That was supposed to be reassuring—but it was not entirely a reassurance, if one knew his mother.

He bowed. She bowed. She smelled like flowers, she always did. She waved a lacy hand toward her desk and went and sat down there, slightly sideways, to face him.

He came closer, folding his hands behind his back, and waited, wondering what kind of report about him could have come in, from what place, and how much trouble he was in.

"So, are you packed, son of mine?" she asked.

"Yes, honored Mother," he said quietly, properly, though sneaking a glance over the papers she had out on the desk. One looked like a building plan. He thought it might be Najida. But it looked different. The rooms were all wrong.

It was, he realized, the new apartment, showing how the rooms were laid out. And she drew from under it another diagram that might be just an enlarged part of that plan, with several rooms attached.

"This is your suite," she told him, and he looked hard, and tried to memorize it on the spot. It was a proper suite, the way he had had at Najida—well, except the hall it opened onto would not be the main hall of the Bujavid, but a hall inside the larger apartment, where there was no hope of getting outside unobserved.

But it had its own sitting room and a second little room for some purpose, and there was a master bedroom and closet, and beyond that a little hall, and a pair of rooms next to the bedroom, each, he decided, with closets. That pair of rooms would be for his aishid.

And she did not take the diagram away. She turned it so he could better see it.

"This will be your suite," she said, and pointed out the numbers on the sides of the room. "These are the dimensions. You will have your own little office, do you see, for your homework."

The extra room was about the size of the closet in the bedroom, but if it was an office, it would be a place for his projects, and that was excellent. His things would not be in danger of being stepped on. And he would have a table. And bookshelves.

"But you do not have enough furniture to fill it, son of mine," she said.

One had supposed furniture would just turn up. Furniture always had turned up. He never had any choice in it.

His mother pulled out another paper and laid it atop the plan, a paper which had official-looking printing and a red stamp with the Ragi crest.

"This is an authorization," she said, "for you to go down to the storerooms."

"Storerooms. Downstairs?" The Bujavid had a lot of levels, and most of them were storage, all the way down to the train station. But he had never been there. Outside the apartment. Outside the apartment was an exciting notion.

"There is a warehouse office on the fifth level, which your aishid will have no trouble finding by this number." She pointed it out, at the top of the paper. "Give the supervisor this paper. I have a copy. You are old enough now to have some notion what you would like. Your father and I thought you might like to apply your own energies to this matter. So in storeroom 15—it says here, do you see?—is your furniture from when you were a baby. Some was damaged in the coup; some was not and has been warehoused since. But one is sure you will have outgrown that. You have the floor plan, with its dimensions, do you see? This will show you what will fit, and you may ask your aishid for their help, but you must *not* show this paper to the supervisor: Everything about the new apartment is classified and not in his need to know. He may see *this* paper, which has the general dimensions." Another paper, with little written on it. "You and your aishid may pick out any furnishings you please. They simply have to fit the space you have."

"Anything?"

His mother briefly held up a forefinger. "Within the bounds of size and taste, son of mine."

"A television?"

"No."

"Honored Mother, it is educational!"

"When one has a good recommendation from your tutor, one may consider it. Not until then."

He sighed. He was not in the least surprised. Even mani had not let him have a television.

"One day, son of mine. Not now. And because you are young, there must be a few other restrictions. You may pick antiquities, but they must be only of metal or wood, nothing breakable, nothing embroidered, and nothing with a delicate finish or patina."

"One has never broken anything! Well, not often. Not in months."

"One trusts you would not willingly be so unfortunate. But if your choice of furnishing is breakable, if it can be stained or easily damaged, it must *not* be an antiquity or a public treasure. And do not overcrowd your rooms, mind. Listen to the supervisor's advice. And note too that a respected master of kabiu will arrange what you choose in a harmony appropriate to the household, so do not give him too hard a task. You will make a list of the tag numbers of those things you wish moved to your suite and deliver that list back to the supervisor. Or you can take back any of your old furniture you would like."

"One would ever so prefer to choose new things, honored Mother!"

"Then do." She handed him the paper and the plan. "So go, go, be about it!"

"Yes, honored Mother!" He sketched a bow and headed for the door at too much speed. Great-grandmother would have checked him sharply for such a departure. He checked himself and turned and bowed properly, deliberately, lest he offend his mother and lose a privilege just granted. "One is very gratified by your permission," he said properly. "Honored Mother."

A very faint smile lay under her solemnity. It was his favorite of her expressions.

"Go," she shaped with her lips, smiling, and gave a little waggle of her fingers.

He left quietly, shut the door, and let a grin break wide as he faced his aishid, fairly dancing in place.

"We get to go down to the storerooms and pick out furniture!" he said. It was the best, most exciting thing since he had gotten here. He held up the papers. "And you can pick, too!"

The papers with the Ragi seal on them meant they had permission to go to the lifts. By themselves. And Lucasi and Veijico, in uniform, had their sidearms with them, and Antaro and Jegari had the small badges which meant Guild-in-training. The guards at the lifts made no objections at all to such a proper entourage, with proper papers. And Lucasi had a lift key, which he used once they got in. "So nobody can stop the lift," he said importantly, as the lift clanked into motion.

They went straight down for a good distance; the lift stopped and let them out in a very officelike corridor that showed other, dimly lit corridors. The place was significantly deserted. Spooky. Their steps echoed.

Lucasi had the paperwork, but did not so much as check it, not since his first look; he said something obscure to Veijico, she said, "Yes, one agrees," and they kept walking down the hall, arriving at the supervisor's office, having contacted the supervisor as they walked.

And the supervisor very politely rose as they entered, looked at the official paper, bowed, then took up a stack of white tags with strings and a little roll of tape, which he brought with him. Veijico gave him the permissible paper with the room sizes. And the supervisor personally led them out and down the hall to a long, long dimly lit side hall, past doors with just numbers on them. He opened the one marked 15 and turned on the lights inside.

It was a huge, dim, cold room full of furniture that made shadows, shadows upon shadows, more than the lights could deal with. The whole room smelled of something like incense, or vermin-poison. And it held the most wonderful jumble of beds and chairs, some items under brown canvas, some just stacked with pieces of cardboard or blankets between.

"One might show you first what is already tagged for you, young lord," the supervisor said.

"One wishes to see it, nadi," Cajeiri said, and followed the man to a set-aside area with a little bureau and a little bedstead and a rolled up carpet. The bureau and the bed had carved flowers. And he almost remembered that bureau with a little favor.

But it was undersized. Baby furniture. It was downright embarrassing to think he had ever used it.

And there were far more wonderful things all around them.

"We are permitted to choose different ones," Cajeiri said.

"That you may, young lord. If one could ask your preferences, one might show you other choices."

"Carving," he said at once. He had seen better carving on a lot of furniture around them, some with gilt, some without. "A lot of carving. With animals, not flowers, and not gold. The most carving there is. You would not have any dinosauri . . ."

The man looked puzzled. "No, nandi. One must confess ignorance of such."

"Well, big animals, then. With trees. Except," he added reluctantly, "we are not permitted to have antiquities."

"I know several such sets," the supervisor said, and led the way far down the aisle between towering stacks of old furniture.

The first set was all right, dusty, but the animals were all gracefully running, more suggestions than real animals. The second one had animals just grazing. That was fine. But not what he wanted.

The third, around the corner, had fierce wild animals snarling out of a headboard and a big one with tusks, staring facc-on from a matching bureau with white and black stone eyes. "This one, nadi!" he said. "And this!"

So a tag went on that set. And he had most of the bedroom. It was a big bed. Bigger than the one he had in mani's apartment.

"You will need chairs for a sitting room, young gentleman; we have a suggestion for seven chairs. And a table. A desk for an office. Carpet for three rooms. All these things."

"And my aishid will have their beds and carpets," he said. "And they can choose for themselves. Whatever they want. But we favor red for ourselves."

"Red. One will strive to find the best," the supervisor said.

There were five wonderful chairs. Mani would approve. They were heavy wood and tapestry that had the most marvelous embroidery of mountains in medallions on the backs and seats, each one different. There was a side table of light and dark striped wood that was almost an antique. And for his office there was a desk that had a picture of a sailing ship, an old sailing ship, with sails. He liked that almost as much as the bedroom set. It reminded him of Najida.

There was a red figured carpet that was fifty years old and hedging on antiquity, too, but the supervisor said if it was in the bedroom, it would surely not be spilled on;

and it was a wonderful carpet, with pictures woven in around the border of a forest and fortresses and animals, with a big tree for most of the pattern, but the bed would cover that.

Then his aishid picked out beds and side tables and chairs for their rooms: Lucasi and Veijico liked plain furniture with pale striped wood, and Antaro and Jegari liked a dark set that had trees and hunting scenes like Taiben forests, and they agreed to mix it up, because Veijico and Antaro had one room and Lucasi and Jegari had the other. But that was all right, too: Mother had said there would be a master of kabiu to sort all that out and put vases and hangings and such that would make it felicitous, however they scrambled the sets.

It was a lot of walking and pulling back canvas covers and looking at things. He thought they would all smell of vermin-poison by the time they got out of the warehouse.

But they were only half done. The supervisor showed them a side room and shelves and shelves of vases and bowls and little nested tables and statues and wall hangings. The supervisor pulled out several hangings he thought might suit, and Antaro wanted a hunting one that he rejected, himself. He took one that was mountains and lakes and a boat on the lake, and Veijico took another that was of mountains, while Lucasi and Jegari took hunting scenes and another mountain needlework.

And there was, in this place, a marvelous hanging that was all plants, and all of a sudden Cajeiri saw what he wanted for the whole room, the whole suite of rooms. "I want that one, nadi," he said. "But I want growing plants, too. I want pots for plants, nadi." He and his associates on the ship had used to go to hydroponics, and nand' Bren's cabin had had a whole hanging curtain of green and white striped plants, and just thinking about it had always made him happy. He suddenly had a vision of plants in his rooms. *His* rooms. And plants were not antiquities, and they could not possibly be outside the rules.

"One will make a note of that, young lord," the

supervisor said, and was busy writing, while Cajeiri peered under an oddly shaped lump of canvas. "One will notify the florists' office."

One was sure it would happen. He paid no more attention to that problem. He saw filigreed brass. And there proved to be more and more of it as he pulled on the old canvas, canvas that tore as he pulled it, it was so old.

The brass object was filigree work with doors as tall as he was, a little corroded and green in spots, and it took up as much room as two armchairs. It was figured with brass flowers that made a network of their stems instead of bars. And it had a brass door, and brass hinges, and a latch, and a floor with trays.

He worked to get all the canvas off.

"That is a cage," the supervisor said. "From the north country. It is, one fears, young gentleman, an antique, seven hundred years old."

"But it is brass, nadi!" He *wanted* it. He *so* wanted it. It was big, it was old, and it was weirder than anything in the whole warehouse. It was the sort of thing anybody seeing it had to admire, it was so huge and ornate. And he wanted it to stand in the corner of his sitting room, whatever it was, with light to show it up, with plants all over. "I am not to have *fragile* antiques," he said. "Brass is different. My mother said I might have brass."

The supervisor consulted his papers. "That exception is indeed made, young lord."

"Parid'ja, nandi," Lucasi said quietly. "In such cages, people used to keep them for hunting. They would go up in the trees and get fruit and nuts. And they would dig eggs. That is what this cage was for. To keep a parid'ja."

"It is wonderful," he said. "One wants it, nadi, one truly, truly wants it!"

"It is quite large," the supervisor said. "It really does not fit easily within the size requirements."

"I still want it, nadi," he said, and put on his best manners. "One is willing to give up two chairs or the table, but I want it. It can even go in my bedroom if it has to."

"In your *bedroom,* young gentleman."

"It can stand in a corner, can it not? I shall give up the hanging if I must. I want this above all things, nadi!"

The supervisor took a deep breath and gave a little bow, then put a tag on the cage and noted it on the list. "One will run the numbers, young gentleman, and assign it a space, if only doors and windows allow."

"We *have* no windows, nadi!" For the first time ever, that seemed an advantage. "And not many doors!"

"Then perhaps it will fit, *with* your chairs and hanging *and* the table. Allow me to work with the problem. One promises to solve it. Meanwhile, search! You may find small items which may delight you."

"One is pleased, nadi! Thank you very much!" He used his best manners. He hurried around the circular aisle, taking in everything. Brass meant he could have old things. He picked out a brass enamelware vase as tall as Lucasi. "For the sitting room," he said.

That was the last thing he dared add. It was big, but it was big *upward,* and it went with the cage. He was satisfied. "May one come back again, nadi," he asked, "if one needs other things?"

"Dependent on your parents' wishes, yes, young lord, at any time you wish to move a piece out or in, we are always at your service. We store every item a house wishes to discard from its possession. We restore and repair items. We employ artists and craftsmen. Should any of these things ever suffer the least damage, young lord, immediately call us, and we will bring it down to the workshop and make whatever repair is necessary."

He bowed, as one should when offered instruction from an elder. "One hears, nadi, and one will certainly remember. But we are very careful! We are almost felicitous nine, we are taught by the aiji-dowager and by our parents, and we are very careful!"

A bow in return. "One has every confidence in your caution, young lord. Rest assured, I shall have staff move these things to the staging area, give them a little dusting

and polish, and you shall have them waiting for you tomorrow."

"Thank you, nadi!" he said with a second bow, and
they all walked back to the entry and took their leave in
the brighter light of the hallway.

He was all but bouncing all the way to the lift, imagining
how marvelous his suite was going to be and where *he*
would put things. *He* would put things. *He* would have a
choice.

He had seen vids about animals. Horses. And ele-
phants. And dogs and cats and monkeys. He had wanted
a horse. And a monkey and a dog and a cat and a bird
and a dinosaur. He had wanted . . . oh, so many things he
had seen in the vids on the ship. But humans had not
brought any of them with them. He had been *very* disap-
pointed that there were no elephanti or dinosauri on
Mospheira.

He thought of things one could keep in a cage like
that. He had instantly thought of several varieties of
calidi, that laid eggs for the table—but calidi were scaly
and had long claws and were not very smart. Parid'ji
were spidery and furry, and moved fast and *ate* eggs. Like
monkeys. He had seen vids. They were a lot like monkeys, but they belonged to the forests, and he had never
thought of bringing one to the Bujavid.

Oh, his whole mind had lit up when they had said the
cage was for that.

And when they were waiting for the lift, where nobody could hear, he stopped and said, "Can you find a
parid'ja, nadiin-ji?"

His aishid looked worried. All of them.

"One can find almost anything in the city market,
nandi," Antaro said. "Or at least—one can ask a mer-
chant to find what is not there. But one is not sure one
should, without permission."

"They are difficult to deal with," Lucasi said. "Your
father would not approve."

"I want one. And you are not to say anything! *Any* of you! I can prove I can take care of it. I have never asked you to do anything secret but this. Find me one, and leave it to *me* that I shall get my father's permission for it. I am his son. He will approve things for me that he would not if you asked him."

There was a second or two of deep quiet. And very worried looks.

"One will try," Antaro said. "One has an idea where one might find a tame one. It may take me a while."

"Then you shall do it," he said as the lift arrived. And ignored the frown Veijico turned on Antaro.

He could hardly contain his satisfaction. He had the cage. He was going to have a monkey. Well, close to a monkey. He had something that was going to be *fun*. And he would have something alive that was going to be *his* and not boring, because it *thought* of things for itself and it was not under anybody's orders.

He had been sad ever since he had had to leave Najida, and sadder since he knew he was going to have to live in a room with no windows and just white paint.

His room would not be all white. His room would be *interesting*. He could not go back into space. But he had his beautiful furniture, he had his own aishid, and he had that beautiful ancient brass cage and he would have a room full of plants like nand' Bren's cabin on the ship. And he would have something to do unexpected things.

He had dreaded the move. Now he could hardly wait.